CATCH TEPIG!

A POKÉMON LOOK & LISTEN SET

BOOK · DVD · HEADPHONES

Watch three episodes of *Pokémon: Black & White*, starring Tepig,
using the collectible Tepig headphones! Read about Tepig in the 32-page book!

Catch Tepig! A Pokémon Look & Listen Set

Your Look & Listen Set comes with a DVD of three action-packed TV episodes and specially designed headphones, all customized to your Look & Listen Set Pokémon!

Publisher: Heather Dalgleish
Writer: Lawrence Neves
Designers: Tyler Freidenrich, Megan Sugiyama, and Katie Stahnke
Art Director: Eric Medalle
Product Development: Drew Barr
Headphone Sculpting: Martin Meunier
Production Management: Jennifer Marx
Production Assistance: Katie del Rosario and Michael del Rosario
Product Approval Manager: Phaedra Long
Product Approval Associate: Katherine Fang
Editors: Michael G. Ryan & Eoin Sanders (for Pokémon) and Ben Grossblatt (for becker&mayer!)

The Pokémon Company INTERNATIONAL

Published by
The Pokémon Company International
333 108th Avenue NE, Suite 1900
Bellevue, Washington 98004 U.S.A.

1st Floor Block 5, Thames Wharf Studios, Rainville Road
London W6 9HA United Kingdom

11 12 13 14 15 9 8 7 6 5 4 3 2 1

Produced by becker&mayer!
11120 NE 33rd Place, Suite 101
Bellevue, Washington 98004 U.S.A.
www.beckermayer.com

becker&mayer!
BOOK PRODUCERS

ISBN: 978-1-60438-159-7

11839

Printed in Hangzhou China, 11/11

Visit us on the Web at www.pokemon.com

Welcome to the world of Pokémon! In this book, you'll learn about their world and the new region of Unova, home to many different Pokémon!

OSHAWOTT

SNIVY

TEPIG

WHAT ARE POKÉMON?

Pokémon are amazing creatures that can be found throughout the different areas in the Pokémon realm! High grasses, swampy marshes, and mysterious forests are all teeming with wild Pokémon, but you can also find them in bustling cities and busy towns. Each species of Pokémon has its own special traits and powers.

Some Pokémon evolve, or grow, into other Pokémon. For instance, Tepig may grow up through training and experience into Pignite, and then later into Emboar. In Unova, Ash sees so many new Pokémon, it makes his head spin!

WHAT ARE POKÉMON TRAINERS?

In the Pokémon world, humans live, work, and play alongside Pokémon. Pokémon Trainers are people who want to make a life's work out of training, befriending, and competing with their Pokémon in Pokémon battles. Great Trainers try their hardest to understand and communicate with their Pokémon through love and friendship.

MEET ASH!

ASH KETCHUM

Ash Ketchum is on a quest to become a Pokémon Master. His journey has taken him to some incredible places and has included lots of adventures! Now in Unova with his trusty Pikachu by his side, Ash moves forward in his mission to be the best Trainer around!

Pikachu, an Electric-type Pokémon, has been with Ash since the beginning, but does not like to travel in a Poké Ball. Instead, it travels side-by-side with Ash, forming a true partnership like no other in the world of Pokémon!

The object Ash is holding is a Poké Ball, one of the special tools of Pokémon Trainers. There's more to learn about them. Turn the page to see!

TRAINER TOOLS

POKÉDEX

The Pokédex is like a digital encyclopedia for Pokémon Trainers. Its vast collection of information makes it one of the most useful tools in a Pokémon Trainer's arsenal.

The Pokédex is also used to record and analyze data on never-before-seen Pokémon, so it's perfect for a region like Unova, where Ash is a newcomer and unfamiliar with the Pokémon living there.

The Pokédex contains a wealth of data about known Pokémon. But a Trainer usually has to see the Pokémon first so that the Pokédex can record the data. Then, the Trainer can use the Pokédex to learn more about it.

XTRANSCEIVER

The Xtransceiver is a new gadget unique to the Unova region. It allows Trainers to call one another and set up battles, and it uses a live video feed so that Trainers can see who's calling.

Pokémon Trainers know that Xtransceiver is pronounced *cross transceiver*.

POKÉ BALLS

Poké Balls are absolutely essential gear for Pokémon Trainers who want to capture and train Pokémon. The Poké Ball is an electronic storage chamber for Pokémon. When Ash wants a Pokémon, he throws a Poké Ball. When it opens, it captures the Pokémon and stores it until released. This is how Ash caught Tepig, Snivy, *and* Oshawott!

There are many types of Poké Balls, and each has a unique purpose and strength. Here are some of them!

A Pokémon Trainer will usually receive several of these right at the start of their adventure, along with a Pokédex! These standard Poké Balls are good for the Pokémon you first meet, but serious Trainers will know all about the other Poké Balls they might come across.

DIVE BALL
Works especially well on Pokémon that live underwater.

MASTER BALL
The best Poké Ball, with the ultimate level of performance. It will catch any wild Pokémon without fail.

NET BALL
Effective in catching Bug- and Water-type Pokémon.

GREAT BALL
Has a higher rate of success in catching Pokémon than the standard Poké Ball.

DUSK BALL
Works much better at night or in gloomy places, like caves.

HEAL BALL
Completely heals the wild Pokémon that it catches, which is great when a Trainer has worn down a Pokémon during an encounter.

ULTRA BALL
Has even higher rates of success than the Great Ball.

LUXURY BALL
Causes Pokémon caught in it to become more attached to their owners.

REPEAT BALL
Effective for capturing Pokémon that have previously been caught once.

Now that you know about Pokémon and the Trainers who battle with them, it's time to follow Ash and explore Unova!

WELCOME TO THE UNOVA REGION!

Ash has started his journey across Unova. He's excited about discovering new Pokémon. He's also got a whole new region to explore and many important people to meet!

The Unova region is filled with colorful cityscapes, lush forests, and forbidding mountain ranges. The people there are just as fascinating as the Pokémon. Pokémon Battle Club managers, rambunctious and exotic Trainers, and even kind-hearted Gym Leaders abound in Unova.

ROUGH WEATHER

Soon after arriving in Unova, Ash and Pikachu witness a strange event. A huge, mysterious thundercloud shooting out weird blue lightning hovers in the sky. Pikachu is zapped and experiences strange effects. Could the cloud have something to do with the legend of Zekrom?

PROFESSOR JUNIPER

The authoritative professor of the Unova region, Professor Juniper is a friend of Professor Oak's and a legitimate force in the world of Pokémon. She researches Unova and its unique Pokémon. Professor Juniper is the one who discovers what's gone wrong with Pikachu's Electric-type attacks.

"Zekrom is a legend in these parts. From within its thundercloud,
Zekrom watches over people and Pokémon."

NEW FRIENDS

Ash befriends two new Trainers and their Pokémon on his journey through Unova!

IRIS

Iris is one of the first people to befriend Ash in the Unova region. She's an active nature-lover who is skilled at gathering fruit from treetops! But don't let her athletic ways fool you. She's all heart and is completely devoted to her Pokémon, Axew.

When Iris first meets Ash, it is under the worst circumstances—Team Rocket is trying to steal her Axew! Ash saves Pidove, Pikachu, and Axew, and Iris realizes that although Ash acts like a kid sometimes, he is completely dedicated to his Pokémon and to all Pokémon in general!

Although Iris is training her Axew, so far it has done little battling. It can use its powerful Dragon Rage move but not with a lot of control.

AXEW

TYPE: Dragon **HEIGHT:** 2'00"
CATEGORY: Tusk Pokémon **WEIGHT:** 39.7 lbs.

Axew uses its tusks to crush berries for food and cut gashes in trees to mark its territory. Its fangs become strong and sharp as they constantly grow back; even if one breaks, a replacement grows in quickly.

CILAN

Along with his two brothers, Cilan is a Gym Leader at the Striaton City Gym. He's a stylish, intelligent opponent whose strength is sizing up the relationship between a Pokémon Trainer and that Trainer's Pokémon.

Cilan is a Pokémon Connoisseur, a title that Ash has never heard of before. After Ash defeats him and wins the Trio Badge, Cilan sees the potential in Ash and asks to join his crew!

Cilan's trusty Pansage is just as good natured as its owner, but it's no pushover. It is a capable and experienced battler.

PANSAGE

TYPE: Grass
CATEGORY: Grass Monkey Pokémon
HEIGHT: 2'00"
WEIGHT: 23.1 lbs.

Pansage lives in the depths of the forest. The edible leaf on its head has stress-relieving properties, and Pansage shares this leaf with tired-looking Pokémon.

ALLIES...

BIANCA

Ash and Iris meet Bianca and her Pokémon, Pignite, on their way to Nacrene City. Bianca was sent by Professor Juniper with a badge case for Ash, but it is stolen by a Minccino. Don't worry—Ash got it back!

MINCCINO

NURSE JOY

Nurse Joy is the name for the entire league of healing women who staff Pokémon Centers throughout the Pokémon world. Pokémon receive the care they need to heal in these Centers. The Nurse Joy in Unova has 16 sisters who are also Nurse Joys in the region.

Nurse Joys usually have helping Pokémon as their assistants. In Unova, it's Audino, which uses sound to diagnose Pokémon.

AUDINO

AND RIVALS!

TRIP

Trip is the first competitor Ash meets in Unova. A very aggressive Trainer, Trip thinks Ash is from the "boonies" and assumes Ash doesn't know anything about Pokémon battling. Ash doesn't get the upper hand the first couple of times they battle. He loses his first battle to Trip because of temporary problems with Pikachu's Electric-type attacks, and then he loses a key five-on-five battle at the Pokémon Battle Club in Luxuria Town. But Trip will get what's coming to him...and soon. Ash is never one to take a defeat lying down!

JESSIE, JAMES, AND MEOWTH

These Team Rocket schemers never stop trying to thwart Ash and his crew, but they usually end up falling far short of their goal of world domination. Still, they persistently go through with some of the most outrageous plans imaginable—all while trying to impress their boss. Although other Team Rocket agents exist, these are the ones who have been a constant thorn in Ash's side.

THE ADVENTURE BEGINS...

...with these three Pokémon!

At Professor Juniper's lab in Nuvema Town, Ash gets to see the three starter Pokémon of the Unova region. In Unova, new Trainers choose their first Pokémon—Tepig, Snivy, or Oshawott!

TEPIG

HEIGHT: 1'08"
WEIGHT: 21.8 lbs.

A Fire-type Pokémon, Tepig can heat things up in a hurry. Tepig is dangerous against Grass types and will battle for you valiantly.

SNIVY

HEIGHT: 2'00"
WEIGHT: 17.9 lbs.

A Grass-type Pokémon, Snivy is quick and intelligent. Snivy learns fast and is an awesome choice against Water-type Pokémon.

OSHAWOTT

HEIGHT: 1'08"
WEIGHT: 13.0 lbs.

A Water-type Pokémon, Oshawott is great when battling Fire-type Pokémon. Oshawott is the one to choose for Trainers who like their battles wet and wild!

To learn more about Pokémon types, turn the page.

POKÉMON TYPES

Pokémon are classified by their type. Some are Grass types, which means they are susceptible to Fire-type attacks, while others are Fire types, which means that Water-type moves would be very effective against them. Water types want to watch out for Electric-type attacks and Grass-type attacks.

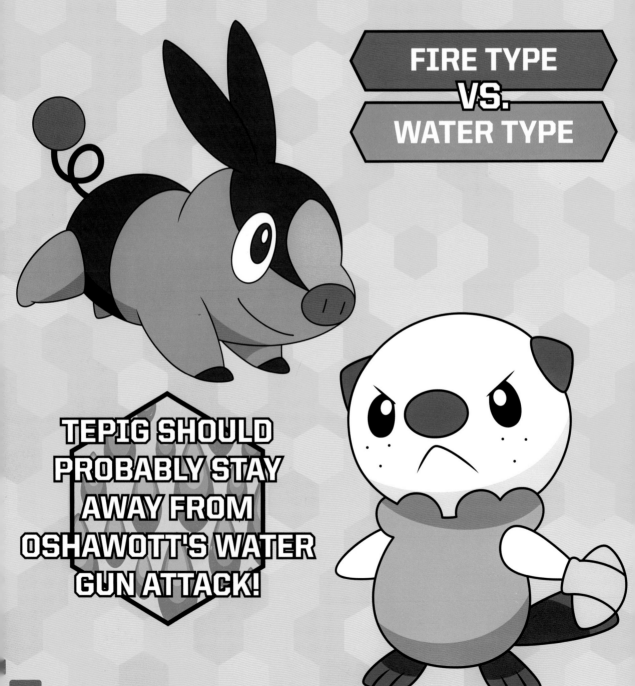

FIRE TYPE VS. WATER TYPE

TEPIG SHOULD PROBABLY STAY AWAY FROM OSHAWOTT'S WATER GUN ATTACK!

THE 17 TYPES

BUG

GRASS

DARK

GROUND

DRAGON

ICE

ELECTRIC

NORMAL

FIGHTING

POISON

FIRE

PSYCHIC

FLYING

ROCK

GHOST

STEEL

WATER

Dual-type Pokémon

Some Pokémon can even be two types at once, like Woobat, which is a Psychic- and Flying-type Pokémon. And when some Pokémon evolve, their Evolutions change types. It's like when Tepig (a Fire type) evolves into Pignite (a Fire- and Fighting-type).

WOOBAT

TEPIG AT A GLANCE

Now it's time to meet a special Tepig that joins Ash on his Unova adventure!

Rumor has it that Tepig's long ears alert it to nearby danger.

Tepig's tail is topped off with a ball. When Tepig is powering up a Fire-type attack, the ball on its tail can glow!

When Tepig isn't feeling well, its snout lets you know—smoke will pour out of it.

Tepig's feet dig in when it's ready to rock! It is able to turn and stop quickly when shooting off moves like Ember.

IT'S ALL IN THE EARS!

Tepig's ears droop when it's sad or sleeping. This is just one way to tell what Tepig is thinking and feeling.

TEPIG

TYPE: Fire
CATEGORY: Fire Pig Pokémon

Tepig uses fire from its nose to roast berries before it eats them.

Tepig uses Ember a lot. It's a basic Fire-type move that sometimes burns an opponent and is especially effective at singeing Grass types.

Ash's Tepig can be stubborn, but what it mostly wants is to please its Trainer. Although not as brash or impulsive as Oshawott, Tepig will not back down from a fight!

Ash's Tepig is a fast learner—and a loyal one, too—but it's also a formidable battler. It can unleash a flurry of fiery moves, which will toast most lightweight opponents right out of the arena.

YOU SAY YOU WANT AN EVOLUTION?

Well, all right! Take a look at Tepig's potential Evolutions!

Tepig starts off strong with a sturdy build and a lovable face, but don't be fooled. This Pokémon was built for strength, endurance, and sheer force!

PIGNITE

TYPE: Fire-Fighting
CATEGORY: Fire Pig Pokémon
HEIGHT: 3'03"
WEIGHT: 122.4 lbs.

Pignite is the evolved form of Tepig. Pignite's food converts into fuel for the flame that burns in its stomach, and when fuel burns in its stomach, its speed increases.

Bianca's Pignite evolved from Tepig, her first Pokémon. Pignite is always eager to battle, but just like Bianca, it sometimes loses its temper when things don't go its way.

TEPIG'S EVOLUTION

EMBOAR

TYPE: Fire-Fighting
CATEGORY: Mega Fire Pig Pokémon

HEIGHT: 5'03"
WEIGHT: 330.7 lbs.

Emboar packs quick, powerful fighting moves, and grows a fiery beard. It uses this beard to set its fists aflame, and then throws blazing punches. Emboar cares deeply about its friends.

With massive fangs and the potential to learn hard-hitting moves like Hammer Arm, this powerfully built brawler is a far cry from little Tepig.

ASH'S JOURNEY BEGINS

The very first town that Ash encounters in Unova is Nuvema Town.

Nuvema Town

This bustling seaside burg is the home of Professor Juniper, who has a variety of Pokémon that she wants Ash to see, including Tepig!

Professor Juniper's Lab

One of the Pokémon available to new Trainers in the Unova region, Tepig is a Fire-type Pokémon. This means that it is quite effective against Grass-type Pokémon and less effective against Water-type Pokémon. Ash first meets Tepig at Professor Juniper's lab, but later rescues a neglected Tepig in Accumula Town.

Ash sees his first Tepig at Professor Juniper's lab. This Tepig looks happy as can be...until Trip passes it over and chooses Snivy as his first Pokémon instead.

THE POKÉMON BATTLE CLUB

The Pokémon Battle Club in Accumula Town is where Ash finds Tepig!

The Pokémon Battle Club is a place for Pokémon Trainers to work out with their Pokémon. Although it doesn't host official Unova League battles, this club offers Trainers the chance to test the strengths and study the weaknesses of their Pokémon.

"Each Trainer enters their Pokémon's profile as well as the type of Pokémon they want to battle against. It's an awesome place for Trainers to sharpen their skills by battling as they see fit!"

WHO IS...
Don George?

Don George is the Battle Manager of the Pokémon Battle Club. Like Officer Jenny and Nurse Joy, he is actually part of a legacy of owners who all look identical. He even shows Ash a picture of his cousins in the Unova region. The Don George in Accumula Town is efficient and respectful. He knows when to stop a battle if a Pokémon is outmatched.

HOW ASH CAUGHT TEPIG

The first Tepig Ash saw was in Professor Juniper's lab, but it wouldn't be his last. In the middle of a battle, something strange happens, and it ends with Ash getting a new Pokémon!

Ash is invited to compete at the Pokémon Battle Club. He uses Pikachu against the Water-type Dewott that is sent out by his opponent. Dewott gets whacked by Pikachu's Iron Tail but comes back with its double-scalchop Razor Shell. An emergency alarm cuts the battle short and eventually leads them to Tepig!

Tale of the Tape

Can a Tepig be mistaken for an Umbreon?

When the security alarm sounds in the Pokémon Battle Club during the Pikachu vs. Dewott battle, Don George's staff informs him that a Pokémon has broken into the food supply in the warehouse. Besides capturing Team Rocket on camera, they catch the fleeting shadow of an escaping Pokémon, which Ash mistakes for an Umbreon, a Pokémon from the Johto region.

Umbreon, the Moonlight Pokémon   Tepig

Ash later finds an abandoned and sickly Tepig. So *that* was the shadow on the security cameras! Ash befriends it and adds another Unova Pokémon to his team!

A Tepig that was left behind by its owner.

Tepig, full of food and filled with confidence!

Not an Umbreon *or* a Tepig. Who could it be?

I CHOOSE YOU! BUT, SOMETIMES, THE *POKÉMON* CHOOSES *YOU*!

Not every Pokémon willingly tags along, as Iris finds out the hard way!

Tepig was rescued by Ash, but Iris has her heart set on Tepig becoming her new Pokémon. Tepig responds with a firm shake of the head that means "I don't think so" as it runs to Ash's side. The same thing happened when Iris tried to claim Oshawott!

WELCOME TO NACRENE CITY!

This awesome battling spot is where Tepig really shines! What is so special about Nacrene City, and what mysteries does it hold?

"Nacrene City is known as the City of Art! The city is also admired for its style, so it's the City of Admiration, too!"

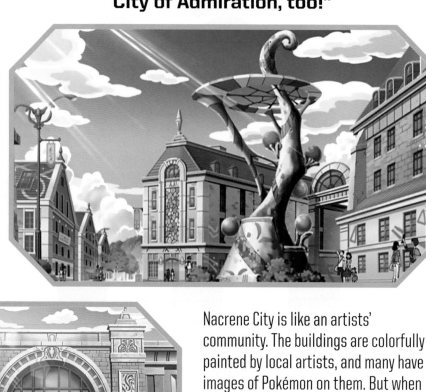

Nacrene City is like an artists' community. The buildings are colorfully painted by local artists, and many have images of Pokémon on them. But when Ash goes to look for the nearby Gym, he finds that the local museum is actually the Gym as well!

Nacrene City Museum

WHO IS... HAWES?

Hawes is the vice curator of the Nacrene City Museum and the husband of the Gym Leader, Lenora. He is a timid man, frightened by what he believes is a haunting in the museum, which turns out to be nothing more than an angry Yamask looking for its mask.

Before Ash can battle at the Nacrene Gym, he's got to do something about the haunted museum. Gym Leader Lenora arrives just in time to help Ash and Hawes solve the mystery of the Yamask mask, but she's not about to battle Ash just yet. Instead, she takes him to the Gym's library to see what he will do. When Ash boldly declares he'll do whatever it takes to get his Gym battle, Lenora can't wait to see how this brash young challenger will do in a two-on-two challenge. Time for Ash's Tepig to make its Gym debut!

This Pokémon is currently part of the Nacrene City Museum catalog of artifacts. Hawes believes it to be a replica, but the Yamask mask is actually a *real* one.

YAMASK

TYPE: Ghost
CATEGORY: Spirit Pokémon
HEIGHT: 1'08"
WEIGHT: 3.3 lbs.

Yamask holds a mask of the face it had in its previous life and sometimes looks at it mournfully.

WHO IS... LENORA?

Lenora is more than just the Gym Leader of the Nacrene City Gym—she's also the curator of the Nacrene City Museum and the wife of Hawes, the vice curator. She is tough and brassy. She doesn't think twice about giving Ash a hard lesson in how to battle, and she uses only Normal-type Pokémon when she battles, which gives her a very flexible style. Ash will learn later that Lenora also has a kind and caring side.

NACRENE GYM BATTLE

Let's look at the first Gym battle that Ash's Tepig fought!

ASH'S TEPIG

VS.

LILLIPUP

Before the battle, Lillipup charms everyone with its cuteness, especially Iris and Pikachu. But once the battle begins, Lillipup is all business!

Tackle
Tackle can be a powerful move. But when Tepig uses it in this battle, Lillipup dodges it.

LILLIPUP

TYPE: Normal
CATEGORY: Puppy Pokémon

HEIGHT: 1'04"
WEIGHT: 9.0 lbs.

The long hair covering Lillipup's face is an excellent radar that senses conditions in the surrounding area.

Take Down

This big move (from such a small Pokémon) turns the tide in Ash's first battle with Lenora. Tepig's Ember does nothing against Take Down, and eventually Tepig falls.

AWESOME COMBO!

Lenora has a really cool trick up her sleeve, and it involves the combination of two moves: Roar and Mean Look.

Roar

Tepig is ready to do battle and singe some fur when suddenly Lillipup uses Roar, which sends Tepig back to its Trainer and brings the next Pokémon in line onto the battlefield.

Mean Look

Obviously not ready, Oshawott is then hit with Mean Look, which prevents its Trainer from switching the Pokémon out for one that is better able to fight. It's enough to throw off any Trainer for the rest of the battle!

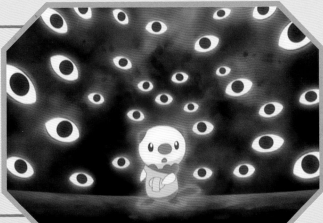

THE REMATCH

After his first match against Lenora, Ash is depressed. Nurse Joy has an idea: a training session with Don George at the Pokémon Battle Club might improve Tepig's skills!

TRAINING SESSION

Thanks to Don George and the Pokémon Battle Club's program, Tepig increases its speed and power. When Lenora and Ash meet for a rematch, Ash is ready!

In Ash's rematch with Lenora, Tepig faces an evolved form of Lillipup called Herdier. Tepig unleashes Ember, but Herdier counters with Shadow Ball. Thanks to improvements made at the Pokémon Battle Club, Tepig is much faster and dodges the attack. But when Lenora resorts to Roar, she forces Tepig to switch out of the battle.

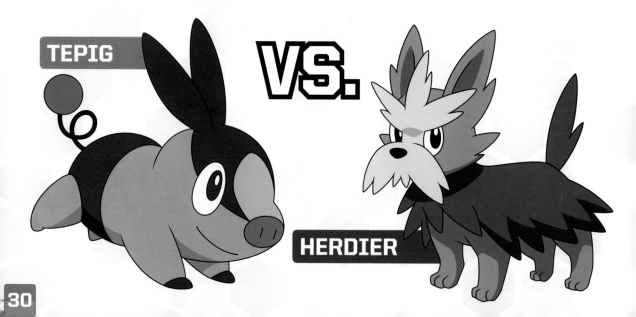

TEPIG

VS.

HERDIER

HERDIER

TYPE: Normal
CATEGORY: Loyal Dog Pokémon
HEIGHT: 2'11"
WEIGHT: 32.4 lbs.

The evolved form of Lillipup. Herdier's hard black fur softens its opponent's attacks like armor.

KEY MOVES IN THE BATTLE

Giga Impact

Herdier uses this move against Tepig. It does great damage, but it leaves Tepig with enough energy to use Flame Charge!

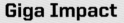

Flame Charge

Tepig learned this powered-up move while training at the Pokémon Battle Club!

VICTORY!

Herdier can't stand up to Tepig's Flame Charge. It's the turning point in the rematch!

The Basic Badge

Ash gains not just Lenora's respect but also the Basic Badge from her Nacrene City Gym!

SECRET MESSAGE!

Complete the words below. Take the letters you added and rearrange them to finish a secret message about Tepig!

Hawe_

Herd_er

_acrene City

Len_ra

L_llipup

_lame Charge

Umbr_on

_oar

Tepig _ _ _ _ _ _ _ _!